The Theme Park of Women's Bodies

T0283041

The Theme Park of Women's Bodies

STORIES

MAGGIE COOPER

BULL★CITY
PRESS
DURHAM, NC

The Theme Park of Women's Bodies
Copyright © 2024 by Maggie Cooper

Library of Congress Cataloging-in-Publication Data

Names: Cooper, Maggie (Fiction writer), author.
Title: The theme park of women's bodies / Maggie Cooper.
Other titles: Theme park of women's bodies (Compilation)
Description: Durham, NC : Bull City Press, 2024.
Identifiers: LCCN 2024004797 | ISBN 9781949344424
(paperback) | ISBN 9781949344431 (epub)
Subjects: LCSH: Women--Fiction. | LCGFT: Short stories.
Classification: LCC PS3603.O582694 T47 2024 | DDC 813/.6--
dc23/eng/20240205
LC record available at https://lccn.loc.gov/2024004797

Published in the United States of America

This is a work of fiction. No identification with actual persons (living or deceased), places, buildings, and products is intended or should be inferred.

Cover photo: Library of Congress, Prints & Photographs Division, Farm Security Administration/Office of War Information Black-and-White Negatives.
Book design: Riley Wojcik and Spock and Associates
Author photo: Ron Cooper

Published by
BULL CITY PRESS
1217 Odyssey Drive
Durham, NC 27713

www.BullCityPress.com

Table of Contents

Furies

Maidens

Crones

FURIES

The Theme Park of Women's Bodies

Welcome to the Theme Park of Women's Bodies! I'm Tina, and I'll be your tour guide today as we explore the park. Before we begin, management requires me to run through a few ground rules: no running, no outside food or drink, and no unauthorized videorecording. Big thanks to InnerBeauty, which sponsors all our park tours—and also allows me to work the counter at their downtown salon on Tuesday and Thursday nights so I can make rent on the apartment I share with three other impoverished feminists!

On to the good stuff: The tour takes approximately half an hour and will end right in front of the entrance to the Miracle of Life, one of our most popular rides, which allows guests to follow an ovum from the moment of conception through the various stages of development and, finally, experience the birthing process through a state-of-the-art twenty-five-foot model of a vagina!

Our first stop on the tour is the historic park entrance, fondly known as the Boob. If you look carefully, you can see that it's topped by a bronze nipple cast from the real-life breast of one of the founders, while the stained-glass areola adds another touch of artistry to this nineteen-story monument to womankind. Can anyone guess the importance of the number nineteen? Yes, you in the GIRL POWER

T-shirt. That's right! The Boob stands as a tribute to the Nineteenth Amendment, which granted women the right to vote. That correct answer gets you one of our limited edition tampom-pom beanies, the perfect feminist fashion statement!

Just over my shoulder, you can see the Boobside stage, where we host a variety show every Friday evening. The program includes an incredible woman contortionist who twists herself into literal knots to accommodate the demands of patriarchal culture, and concludes with the entire cast performing a rousing rendition of Shania Twain's classic "Man, I Feel Like a Woman."

Follow me to your right, where we'll see some of the historic features of the park, including the Tower of Flaming Corsets, which is lit every evening at dusk, and the Second Wave, one of the park's only water features, where you can cool off after a hot day of sightseeing. Those of you who signed up online will come back here for our virtual reality experience *Roe Revived*, which transports visitors back to a time of legal abortion in all fifty states and allows participants to practice guiding abortion seekers through crowds of protestors rendered in highly accurate 3D. At the end of the experience, don't miss the opportunity to sign up for six months free access to RED, a period app that definitely isn't tracking your data in order to sell it to pro-life organizations!

As we pass over the River of Menses, make sure to admire the lovely tributary of blood and cellular debris that threads through this area of the park. For those of you in the mood for something romantic, I recommend a gondola ride with one of our all-women team of gondoliers, several of whom are former members of the U.S. women's soccer team. Would you believe that their compensation packages at the park rival their league earnings? As an employee myself, I can attest to the fact that's not because our salaries here are particularly impressive! Dental insurance is a sticking point with management, and although I've been asked not to discuss it on the tour, if you're interested in supporting staff efforts to organize, you can find us at @ourbodiesourunion on all social platforms.

How did I get this job? Well, as my parents helpfully point out to me every time I talk to them on the phone, the career prospects for a women and gender studies major with visible facial piercings are somewhat limited. I tried bartending, but the visitors here are much more appreciative of my fun facts. For example: did you know that Elizabeth Cady Stanton, who is celebrated as one of the leaders of the suffrage movement, also campaigned against extending the vote to Black Americans? The failure to think intersectionally has long been a feature of the women's movement, something that we can see today in the prevalence of so-called gender-critical feminism and the persistent centering of able-bodied, upper-middle-class, cis white women in conversations about access to reproductive health. What's that? You're wondering about the crash that just came from behind the Roller Coaster of Women in Politics? I'm sure that's just the ride soundtrack, which culminates with the cacophonous shattering of the glass ceiling! Now let's move along. No time to dilly-dally!

Can everyone hear me? People often ask why there's no Theme Park of Men's Bodies, and while I can't answer that question for you, I can tell you that, in the U.S., women are almost five times more likely than men to be victims of sexual assault. What a number, right? The Land of Sexual Violence is currently closed for the installation of several new rides, including a bumper boat feature in which visitors are buffeted by the winds of public opinion as they attempt to navigate the choppy waters of the #MeToo movement. You would think the fact that the park is investing in a major expansion would mean that budgets might support adequate sick pay, parental leave, and professional development for staff; however, I'm sorry to say that isn't the case, and cuts to the employee roster mean that most of us are now working not just metaphorical but literal double shifts.

Everyone stand to the right for a moment, please. It looks like Officer Patty, our Chief of In-Park Security, is making her way toward the entrance, so be sure to give her a wave! Looks like she's in a bit of a hurry today.

Any questions? Yes, I do see that smoke rising over the tower of the Tower of Female Empowerment. No, I do not think it's any cause for concern. Thanks to Patty, security inside the park is very good, and while I know that you may have read about the protests last week, I can assure you that reports have been wildly exaggerated. The staff of the Theme Park of Women's Bodies is committed to peaceful negotiation with all stakeholders, and the only violence occuring at the park is the violent erasure of the experiences of Black and Brown women, trans folks, and other people from marginalized backgrounds.

Now, due to schedule constraints, we'll be skipping over our penultimate stop at the Ferris Wheel of Sex and Sexuality, and instead moving toward the Miracle of Life ride, where I will conclude the tour. It looks like the line is nice and short today, so you'll be journeying down the fallopian tube in no time! Here's another fun fact: the U.S. maternal mortality rate is currently three times higher for Black women when compared to their white counterparts. Fortunately, this ride will satisfy visitors of all races and ethnicities, having been named one of the tri-state area's best off-the-beaten-track attractions for the past three years in a row!

At this time, I'll ask any cis white men, individuals with a net worth of over $500K, and anyone who follows J.K. Rowling on social media to step to this side, where we'll make sure that you are first up for our most popular ride. Ma'am, I'm going to have to ask you to get back into line, please. Once visitors have entered the ride perimeter, we cannot allow them to exit. Everyone buckled up and ready to go? Wonderful! A little smoky smell is perfectly normal, nothing to worry about at all. You're all going to enjoy this so very much! And if—when!—you emerge at the other end, I guarantee you're going to have a newfound appreciation for the Miracle of Life.

The rest of you—I see we're a rather small group—feel free to take one of these signs I'm handing out and make your way back to the Boob to join the peaceful demonstration. Thanks so much for joining me on this tour of the Theme Park of Women's Bodies, and don't forget to exit through the gift shop to browse our full line of souvenir menstrual cups!

Operation Hecuba

Operation Hecuba was launched in the summer of 2052, when the energy crisis was in full swing. At that point, even the big cities—New York, London, San Francisco—were graying out at least once a day due to shortages. It wasn't a new idea; for years now, the scientific community had discussed the potential for human emotions to generate energy the grid so obviously craved. After all, hadn't feeling proved more consistent and more reliable than our rational modes of thought? There was debate as to how, exactly, to proceed from this thesis. Would it be parental love that proved the most electric? Would the night light up with the power of hope?

The answer: of course not. From the most preliminary tests, it was clear that the feelings that had the most potential to generate an electrical current were negative ones. Righteous fury proved to be the most effective of the various subcategories. Frustration tended to burn out too quickly, and guilt seemed to weaken the current.

In the literature, which preferred more neutral terminology, they were called the subjects, but in the press, they had other names: the generatrixes, the Hecubites or, simply, the women. For as the early tests had gone on, it had become clear that, on average, women were by far the more effective generators. Men were unreliable, too quick to flare up and peter out. The electrical charge of a woman wronged—that was what the world needed. And so, the decision was made that this, like so much else, would be woman's work: the work of lighting up the world again.

The layout of the plants was relatively simple. Wide open floors were filled with what the literature referred to as workstations, but what the women themselves called Hellboxes: enlarged cubicles where they strapped themselves into harnesses and headsets, affixing wires to key pressure points. There were screens where the women could track their output and simulations they were encouraged to run—series of images, conversations, videos that might incite the sort of righteous anger that made the generators hum to life.

Shifts were structured as eight-hour blocks, with two hours on and one hour off: the analytics indicated that sustaining anger for any longer than two hours at a time was tricky, resulting in peaks and valleys of energy that required too much recalibration. It was exhausting, but in time, the subjects found that summoning up a slow, steady burn became as familiar as filing expense reports or grading math tests or performing titrations. One could, perhaps, get used to anything.

When the first plant had opened, there were concerns—history repeats itself after all, and hadn't we both asked and then ultimately ignored the same questions about nuclear power? What were the long-term effects on the subjects? On the rest of the population? Was there danger of spillage? Did anger radiate? Would we be able to tell if it did?

Yet as it became clear that Operation Hecuba would be effective, public response took on an overwhelmingly positive tone. Who could complain about more power, fewer grayouts? A chance at the kind of quality of life that our parents had enjoyed before the first Outage? The Department of Energy was delighted with the results, and in year four, Dr. Maisie Els, who had been placed in charge of the operation, won an open seat in the Senate. It was, the press reported, a brilliant solution: no toxic waste and a far smaller carbon footprint than either coal or natural gas. A boost to employment rates in areas where well-paying opportunities were few and far between.

In the early days, women sometimes traveled across state lines in order to try out for one of the facilities. It was the rare job with no educational requirements—admission rested entirely on your performance in the testing and a brief psychological exam. As far as the public knew, there had been no problems thus far, but Dr. Els and her team went on the record to say that, while some candidates might be particularly prolific in energy production, a certain level of emotional stability was key to long-term viability of the project.

The women were housed on-site in dormitories and encouraged to devote their off hours to activities like meditation and yoga. Visits home were permitted once a week, although the longer the women worked at the plants, the less frequently they chose to take advantage of them. Psych evaluations and wellness activities notwithstanding, it was punishing to live inside anger day in and day out. Some women quit, but others embraced the feeling: dark with purple edges, like the most vibrant kind of bruise, pressed over and over.

By year five of the program, there was at least one plant in every state, with almost 1,200 across the country. Hellboxes were installed in old schools and retail fulfillment centers and warehouses. Energy flowed into the grid. Dr. Els was elected to a second Senate term and awarded honorary doctorates by prestigious universities.

In the plants themselves, the women had begun to organize. As they grew used to the work, they could fill their off hours not just with meditation and with yoga, but with reading, whispers. They powered the country from coast to coast: how could they fail to recognize the scope of their power? Their fury could light up a city. Their indignation powered office buildings and medical labs and digital printing facilities and coffeemakers. They had buried their hearts deep, but now they dug them up and peeled back the layers, showing one another the sources of their anger: here, he hit me; here, he left her crying; here, they never listened; here, I found her pulpy, battered, dead.

Together, they would write a new history, in which one witch is burned, but many witches make the world burn around them. Hot, bright: the power lines still strung up above rural highways, deep underground where the subways ran, in the White House where wires connected security cameras, computers, the reading lamp over the president's desk. In their rage, the women were a barely controlled flame. They were a forest fire. They were the crackling heat of hell itself, come back to light it all up, then burn it all down.

Our Lady of the High Seas

The pirates had found each other first on land, in the dim back room of a pub rank with brine and ferment:

Talia, the first mate, with her sparkling collection of daggers and dexterous fingers—the one to write their ship's papers and forge the hand of the king.

Soo, the biggest and the strongest, whose arms first raised the sails to the west wind.

And Mergareta herself, who burned bright against the dinge of the port city, who had been born with a webbing between her two smallest fingers as if she had been made for life at sea.

She told the others that she'd taken the purse from a princeling in a city to the west, left him buck naked between silk sheets—a pretty story, though Talia and Soo knew it for a half-truth, purpled like the bruises that showed where Mergareta's neck met her shoulders. No matter. The magic of coin was in its alchemical properties: the ease with which it became a tall mast and sails, a stern and bow—shabby but seaworthy.

They christened the ship Our Lady, after the holy virgin and the old crone on the dock who had cackled when she saw the three women striding toward the boat yard with a heavy coin purse and no man. Our Lady after the mothers they had left back on the mainland weary and smiling—or the mothers who had left them first. Our Lady after Mergareta, who wielded her pistol with all the cold grace of a queen.

Even she was surprised at the speed with which the crew of Our Lady filled their vessel. At each port, there was at least one good woman waiting for her chance to come aboard and take the vow of the pirate wenches. Soon, the decks shone with swabbing, and a newly sewn sail flapped proudly from the mast. There were wool blankets and fresh coffee liberated from plump trading vessels, plenty to eat, and grog on special occasions. There were songs from Soo's homeland to the south, a fiddle, and a few crew members who could carry a tune.

They wanted for little, and yet there was no denying that to pledge themselves to the life aboard ship had meant giving things up: the shade of tall trees and the taste of fresh strawberries and mint, Sunday morning walks with papa and the false and heady hope that the right man might one day make his way up the goat path into the little village. Tiny fingernails and tiny toes swaddled in soft flannel.

But oh, to see what they had gained: the salt air in their lungs, the sight of the sun rising off the prow of their ship, the joy they took in their bodies and in one another. And then, much to their surprise: a child they might all share, borne in the belly of the one among them who had lived most easily as a man, who had scrabbled aboard the ship between drawn blades only to croak out the Oath:

I swear now or am else foresworn: a woman's place is on the seas, and pirates-in-arms live only for each other.

When Thomasena made her squalling, screeching entrance, it was below the clear blue skies and amid a circle of pirate souls, with Mergareta herself standing by to pull and rinse and swaddle. The little one grew up in the little cabin below the prow, less little every day—taller, stronger, more a pirate. And so the ship became Our Lady after Thomasena, too. From that first morning, what had begun as a simple means of escape became a mission: to keep the ship sound enough that Thomasena might one day set the sails toward her own freedom.

They did not call themselves mothers; no, that was what they had left behind on the shore. But they were her pirates, and between their blades and their hands and their hearts, she was fiercely protected, cared for, loved as much as any land-child.

Thomasena's first word was *captain*, and when she took her first steps across the deck, the pirates cheered and sang and cracked open a cask of the finest rum. When she tasted it, she cried, and her pirates laughed and dried her tears and told her that someday, things would be different.

As the years passed, other ships learned to steer clear of the vessel, which took on new names with each port of call: the Lady's Ship, the Sirens' Ship, the Ship of Roses. They captured and they plundered, and once a month, they raised a red flag, set anchor, and floated as the moon rose swollen and blazing in the sky over the mast. Before setting sail once more, they swabbed the decks with blood, and the wood ran slick, the air rich and heavy with iron. Afterward, as they emptied their buckets into the sea, sharks circled the bow, and Mergareta sang to them in the vicious, flowing language of her people.

The crew heard the tales at ports from Galilee to Guangzhou. Some younger sailors scoffed at the notion of a ship packed with women, while others, cackling lewdly, spun colorful tales of the orgies that took place aboard.

They were not all wrong, of course. The sea would be a lonely place were it not for skin on skin and lips on lips and lips on skin in the swaying of the hammock or the hot press of a cabin. It was discovered early on that there was great demand for objects of certain proportions, and when a raid took place, the pirates took care to seize the candlesticks and such like. As the captain, Mergareta had her choice of the women aboard ship, but she chose carefully. Soo was the opposite; there were only a very few members of crew who had not had her tongue on their nether regions, and in those cases, it was never for lack of opportunity.

Talia kept to herself until, at one frigid northern port, a stout redhead with close-cropped locks came aboard and took up the mantle of ship's doctor. In the next skirmish, Talia took a blade to the thigh and found her way under the new doctor's hands and then into the new doctor's bed, from which she didn't return for the duration of the winter.

When she grew old enough, Thomasena watched it all with amusement, running to the galley for a piece of hardtack and sweet honey and a bit of gossip about who was seen in whose hammock, who had fallen out over the division of some new spoils. Though she was the only child on board the ship, she was never lonely, learning to tie knots from old Peg or fishing off the prow with quiet Alice.

And yet, they should have known that a girl born to the waves would have her own desires. Thomasena knew the ship and the tide and the sun and the moon, but her feet longed to know what it was like to walk a street or climb a mountain. She had heard their stories of the land, good and bad: the strawberries and mint, the little house at the edge of the village, the glittering ballroom of the great palace. The men, the men, the men.

Thomasena longed for it all and, finally, on her nineteenth birthday, a ship's meeting was held, and a decision made by the provisions laid out in the ship's charter. A debate, followed by a vote, tallied on the official ledger.

Though discussion beforehand had been split, the vote was nearly unanimous. Thomasena would walk on land, if that was what she wanted, for, as Mergareta said in a tone both fierce and gentle:

The day this ship becomes a prison is the last day you will call me captain of Our Lady.

On the day they took Thomasena into harbor, Talia presented her with a book bound in the skin of old enemies: the story of Our Lady and its crew, recorded over many weeks of candlelit evenings. Thomasena cried as she kissed each pirate goodbye, tasting the salt of their skin on her lips as she made her way down the gangplank.

MAIDENS

The Cure

When we first entered the soaking chamber, we drew back at the sight of those awful hoses, the many knobs. We had imagined a still pond, a shallow pool, something altogether more inviting. What we found was stark tile, a fleet of doctors all in white. Perhaps we should have known; there is something wrong with each of us. The waters are the cure, and cures are not always pleasant.

We soak two hours in the morning and two after lunch, gazing up at the cathedral ceiling as our limbs grow heavy, sodden. We are rich and poor, beautiful and homely: lithe Baroness Aurelie, with her jewels and her temper; frail Clothilde, who has come on the nuns' charity; sweet Frieda from the mountains, in her fine embroidered frock. We are, all of us, of childbearing age, and yet we have failed to bear what is expected. So we soak, and after, we go to the mirrors that hang in our bare rooms, where we study our own faces.

Change is slow, but when it comes, we see it. Ears, lips, noses—the parts of ourselves that we once learned to recognize. They erode slowly, washed smooth by the water, so that we seem to blend together. The doctors mistake our names: Aurelie for Clothilde, Clothilde for Frieda.

The water, they tell us, is not for drinking, but we sneak tastes. If this is what it can do to the outsides of us, what will happen when we take it in? At first we recoil at the taste of iron and sulfur, but in time, we long for the bitter weight of metal on our tongues.

After dark, we steal back to the tubs and twist the knobs ourselves, watching as our new reflections ripple. We drink long and deep from the taps, and inside, we feel a stirring. Sediments accrue on chalky surfaces, surfaces we can't see, but feel with senses we didn't know we had until we came here. Our bellies swell with something harder, heavier than flesh, and the doctors whisper. They do not know what comes next.

The babies are dense and pewter-colored, their features sharp, distinct. They do not cry, but we hold them to our smooth breasts and wait patiently. In the morning, we wail as the doctors uncurl our fingers from the babies' mineral wrists. We lie in our spare white rooms and taste the iron in our tears, until the doctors take us by the hand and lead us back to the tubs again.

We have come to take the waters, but in the end, it is they that do the taking. This is the cure: when the doctors turn their backs, we sink low, under the water. We dissolve like powder, like sugar, like salt.

After the photograph Hydrotherapie, Friedrichsbad, Baden Baden, Germany, 1999, *from* Water Rites *by Lucinda Devlin*

Red Cherry

I'm approximately 105 days pregnant and lying in bed thinking about what I would order at Cook Out. It's one way of tuning out the heavy breathing of White Sara on my right, the barely perceptible sound of the bass in Puerto Rican Sara's earbuds on my left, and the rush of the AC vent above me pushing back the sticky North Carolina August. I know from Googling that the Cook Out is 1.4 miles away, next to a strip mall with a Marshall's, a Planned Parenthood, and a vacuum repair store called—no kidding—Sucks to Be You.

Google is allowed at the Motherhood Project, though it isn't encouraged. The nurse who runs our Expectant Mothers group tells us that the internet is not our friend when it comes to trustworthy medical information and we should instead "use our resources." My resources, like those of our dying planet, are limited. They consist, mainly, of a three-year-old Samsung Galaxy phone with (thank god) a generous data plan and what my ninth grade social studies teacher once called my "excellent critical thinking skills." This was the same ninth grade social studies teacher who assigned group projects on world famine and global warming and pretended not to notice when I did the whole PowerPoint myself.

The group project here is giving birth, whether you like it or not, and if it were graded, I suspect I would be barely passing. I got all As in ninth and tenth grade and then, after sophomore year, I grew boobs and stopped doing my homework, so my performance here is consistent with that trend.

At Cook Out, my order varies depending on my mood, but it always involves a red cherry shake and a side of onion rings. Sometimes, I'll go steak-style burger with extra A1; other times, BBQ sandwich. Occasionally, I'll do a corn dog, although my best friend Jessie would say that a corn dog is what got me in this situation in the first place. My other friend Emily would say that's crude, and she would be right, but that wouldn't keep us all from laughing about it.

Jessie and Emily have been texting and, once, they came by to drop off a package with a cute maternity top and a slice of my favorite chocolate cake from Indulge! at the mall where Jessie works, but I have a feeling that they've started another thread that's just the two of them, un-pregnant and planning where to go out on the weekend or bitching about their bosses the way the three of us used to. I can't really complain. I'm the one who hasn't been responding to most of the messages they do send, but it still feels kind of shitty to know they are talking without me.

When I'm done thinking about what I would get at Cook Out, I imagine walking around the aisles of Marshall's and, oftentimes, that's enough for me to drift off, a gentle pan over the rows of leggings and shirts and stuff that I would pick up and look at but never buy. In my imagination, I have a cart, but there's only one thing in it—a trick that Jessie taught me when we used to go to stores just to get out of the heat but didn't want the employees to think we weren't serious about actually buying something. It only works the first few times, but then we would find a new store and try again there, and eventually the summer would be over and we'd go back to school, where the spluttering old AC kept the building at a sweaty 80 degrees or so.

This is one perk of the Motherhood Project, at least— there is excellent air conditioning, the kind that makes the hairs on my arms stand on end while we sit in Expectant Mother classes and watch videos that all seem to be variations on the same theme: How to Feed Your Baby, How to Burp Your Baby, How to Change Your Baby, each starring a blond actress with raccoony eye makeup who acts like she has never actually seen a baby before. One afternoon during our allotted hour of computer time, Puerto Rican Sara Googled the actress and discovered that after the baby videos, she had been in several softcore porn videos, only one of which was available to stream online, and then, only for $9.99, which no one was willing to pay.

We are all either saving our money for when the babies come and we get to leave the Motherhood Project for our regular lives again, or we don't have any money to save in

the first place. Really, most of us are in the second cate-
gory, although White Sara had told me that she had heard
that Shayla's family owns a car dealership in Raleigh and
the only reason she's here is that the nicer place you had
to pay for kicked her out for sneaking out to see her boy-
friend—who was not, Sara somehow knew, the same as
Shayla's baby-daddy. Shayla was keeping her baby because,
she said, the adoption system was prejudiced against Black
babies. Her parents were going to raise her kid so that
she could go back to college, she said, although she also
said that she wasn't going back to college but instead to
LA where she had "some gigs lined up." I am skeptical. I
am not going to keep my baby because I both can't afford
to and don't want to, and part of the reason I am at the
Motherhood Project in the first place is because the flyers
promised "expert assistance navigating the adoption system to make sure your child is placed with a happy family
who will allow him or her to thrive."

If I am going to have a baby, it seems irresponsible to
not at least attempt to figure out what to do with it—I
can't not think of it as "it," even after seeing the ultra-
sound and seeing my stomach swell and thinking, proba-
bly more than I should, about how I could be incubating
the next Adolf Hitler underneath my increasingly tight
BITE ME T-shirt. Last week at my appointment, the doctor
asked me if I wanted to know the sex, and I said no, but
when the nurse went into the hall to check on another pa-
tient, I looked at my chart and found the place where she
had circled FEMALE.

Lying in bed between the Saras, I can almost taste the
red dye number two and feel the grease of the onion rings
on my fingers. 1.4 miles isn't really that far for a reason-
ably healthy eighteen-year-old, even a pregnant one, even
with the humidity of August in North Carolina. Could the
hit of pure sugar and salt be enough to get me past the
mean Christian ladies holding signs with pictures of dead
babies on them? I know that abortions (a word that has
never been spoken aloud at the Motherhood Project) ar-
en't exactly a breeze, but the same could be said for five
more months of pregnancy, followed by labor, followed
by an entire lifetime of my future child being potentially a
serial killer or a totalitarian dictator or maybe just a perfectly nice person, but a perfectly nice person who puts
even further strain on our planet's natural resources and
contributes to the onset of climate crisis.

If I had the baby, would I take her to Cook Out and order her a red cherry shake? Tell her that the reason she ex-
ists is because I let some corndog pop my cherry? Would
I have to share my onion rings—a precious, limited natural resource? Would she grow up to say snarky teenager
things like Sucks to Be You, *you win some, you lose some*, BITE
ME, mom? Would it be like a group project with just the
two of us—her and me driving through the drive-through
again and again, licking salt and grease from our fingers,
eating until our stomachs stretched and domed? Would
she like it?

The City

In the City of Ladies, the skyscrapers have breasts, firm perky ones whose nipples harden in the chill of winter. No one thinks much of it because everyone in the City of Ladies has breasts, and although some still choose to wear brassieres, they are considered purely optional, even a little retro, with their wire clasps and shining eggshell cups.

In the City of Ladies, the preferred mode of greeting is a graceful curtsy and, as a result, the sidewalks are filled with bobbing heads and breasts, especially on Tuesday afternoons, which is when everyone goes to the open-air markets for watercress, red meat, and broth. This is what is eaten in the City of Ladies: sirloin steaks and lamb loins seared at high heat, peppery watercress salad, clear and subtle soups.

In the City of Ladies, there is no alcohol, only water, still and sparkling, which is served in fancy glasses, chilled to precise temperatures, by bartenders wearing soft white kidskin gloves. In the City of Ladies, everyone wears gloves, of course, to protect the delicate skin of their hands, and there is no hard labor in the City of Ladies, only corporate event planning and editorial design and food styling.

There is no grime in the City of Ladies, and no crime either, only rhyming poetry and none of the nasty aftereffects of industrialization. The City of Ladies has been gently urbanized, without overcrowding or tenement housing or sewers. Of course, it wasn't always this way, but in the City of Ladies, long memories are not cherished. To be a maiden is to forget.

Yet not all the maidens are as forgetful as they might be and, every year, some are chosen to leave the City of Ladies. Most know their time is coming. A few, having studied the books of myths, seek male companionship or procreation. Others carry the old ways in their bodies: a soreness of muscles, the taste of strong drink on their tongues. A few feel suffocated, strangled by the weight of breasts that have never seemed entirely their own. But there are always one or two that are caught unawares, not knowing that they are the gristle in the meat, the fleck of dirt in the fresh green of salad. They must be told, in a tone smooth yet firm. Each year, the ladies who are in charge of such things escort them to the filigree gates of the City, which are tall and strong, locked tight against the world beyond.

When the gates are opened, there is an exchange. The newcomers have been waiting; they have traveled long and far to seek admittance. They are given gloves, escorted to filmy-curtained suites to refresh themselves. They are fed suppers of watercress and steak tartare, and their brassieres are unhooked, discarded. They smile nervously at one another and lift chilled glasses in a toast. It is dusk, and outside in the City of Ladies, the breasts of the skyscrapers glow rosy against the sunset.

CRONES

The Island

I.

It's an old story: the Roman legions, the village burned, the women raped and drowned in the lake where they had washed their underthings. The little girl left on the shore, untouched, alone.

Her name was Christiana Elena, and even before the legionnaires came, the elders had said there was something about this one. In her fourth year, when she had left her mother's lap to sit with the older children on the far side of the fire, great-grandmother had pointed to the girl's kneecaps, rounded and smooth. *Lucky*, the old woman had said, in a voice cracked with age and unknowing. It was only three years later that Christiana Elena was gathering berries on the far side of the lake, her basket nearly full, when she smelled the smoke. She ran out to the beach and stood, blessed kneecaps caked with dirt as the village burned before her.

It was night before she made her way into the water, tasting ash in her mouth as she swam toward the lake's center. There, the bodies floated—aunt, sister, mother. She clung to them. Dawn came, and the sun rose over the swell of flesh: an island.

At first, there was only silence, but by the time the day grew hot, the insects buzzed among the limbs and torsos.

Birds cried out overhead, and in one, Christiana Elena heard the voice of great-grandmother.

She stayed, catching fish in a net made from the hair of her middle sister, eating the mushrooms that sprang up from her aunt's fingernails, the soft greens that grew between her eldest cousin's toes. Her mother's body became the first house: sad brown eyes the windows, and the sweet curve of her shoulder a bed to sleep in. An earlobe for a pillow, a knuckle for a spoon. Amid such fullness, she could almost forget she was alone.

II.

As the legionnaires marched farther and wider, the others began to arrive—the other girls who had been wily or strong or stubborn or mostly just lucky. A dark-haired girl leading a cow heavy with calf; a thin-faced girl with only eight fingers; a girl in what they called a boy's body with streaks of blood and dirt lacing her back. In their first nights, they shivered and rocked, cried out against remembered pains but, in time, the water calmed them, lapping up against their memories until their dreams ran clear.

There were no new bodies. These girls had traveled too far for the dead to follow, except in dreams. Even so, the island grew around its new inhabitants, stretching across the center of the lake in an alchemy of flesh turned to soil. Lanes sprouted along the paths of veins and arteries. A grove of thighbones grew into saplings. A garden of thumbs and fingers bloomed. And then, before long, a body politic: a council to keep the peace, to minister to the sick, to soothe the melancholy. A chorus of voices to sing the nightmares away.

The day that Christiana Elena died, the rest of the founders joined hands and made a ring around the island, where they stood for ten days and ten nights, growing still and quiet. Their bodies became the wall, a way to protect the place they had created: a place where bodies are not buried, a place where they become.

III.

Why have you come here? We all have our reasons. The legionnaires are not the only ones for whom the body is a vessel to be spilled. It is by their hands that the island grows, each new arrival a departure from a place where *lucky* can only mean *gone*.

We sighted you on the shore, pacing the same beach where Christiana Elena stood with her perfect kneecaps. We saw ourselves in your cracked lips, your bruised forearms.

Step in now. These boats are the cupped hands of our sisters. We will paddle you home with oars made of sterna and scapulae.

This is no paradise: we sweat and we hunger; our bodies ache and they slow. But when the wind blows, we sing along with the songs of our foremothers, and when the rain falls, we taste their tears on our cheeks. And so we stay, until our bodies learn the curve of the shoreline. Until our thighbones arch into bridges, our elbows harden into the knobs of doors. Trace the ribs of the island wall and feel its strength beneath your fingers.

Will you join us? When you are ready, lie down to rest. Let the purslane sprout in the soft down of your cheek as the water plays against your hairline. Let the cows graze on the nape of your neck. Let your eye become a wishing well, your teeth become a stairway. Let your tongue become the path that will lead the next woman home.

A Lesbian's Guide to Cave Exploration

There is nothing, Lois says, gayer than spelunking.

Kaoli rolls her eyes as she smooths her hair back into a long, heavy ponytail. Don't tell my husband.

It is a joke, but in some ways, Lois isn't wrong: here we are, a group of women in cargo pants and loose canvas shirts standing in the gaping mouth of a cave, making our way in through narrower and narrower passages, running calloused hands against smooth walls—dripping, cool, and ancient. A group of women in the dark, holding onto one another as we make our way deeper.

We're a good team: Sasha, with her uncanny sense of north and south; Lois, pushing us to go longer, further; Kaoli, making sure we always have Band-Aids, snacks, and a few nips of whiskey just in case. I am the one who listens to the cave noises, pays attention to the skittering of a mouse, the scrape of rubber soles on stone.

Our headlamps shine over rock formations, and our boots weather in the damp as we trace new paths, shimmy through tight spaces. With my little-boy hips, I was built for this. Sasha has to turn sideways and squeeze to make her way through certain passages.

There are maps, of course; we are not the first explorers. But the caves are as alive as we are, and more often than not, the maps must change. What was once an opening becomes a wall of gravel, impassable; what was once blocked opens onto the next room. Are we not all the same? Breathing, changing; a collection of open doors and closed passageways.

The men who came before us—one hundred, two hundred years ago—did not hesitate to put their mark on the landscape. We find steel beams and abandoned tools, an old lantern, the bones of a chicken dinner on a ledge. We move like ghosts in the darkness, leave no trace. Or no: the only trace that we leave is one you can't see, the one we leave on each other.

Lois is the leader, so it is fitting that she is the one to raise the question. When will we stop this halfway game of dipping in and coming back up for air, these long weekend expeditions that end back at a half-paved parking lot. When we will go for good?

There is a silence, and I listen to the hush of the cave, under which I can almost hear our four hearts beating: today, today, today, today. Then Kaoli shakes her head, her hair like a horse's tail. I notice the first threads of silver in the thick black.

I'm not ready, she says, and though Sasha nods along, I want to protest: how much longer? I've started to feel an ache in my knees some days, a creaking like the slow movement of rock.

Maybe we're as ready as we'll ever be—ready to leave behind the safety of packed lunches and sunlight on our necks, the car radio on the way home. We don't discuss it again but, sometimes, when Lois is leading, I can see a hint of something in her eye, and I want to chase it.

Instead, Kaoli makes gorp—good ol' raisins and peanuts, but different every time: good ol' almonds or dried mango or chocolate chips. The longer we stay out, the stranger it tastes—the more I struggle to decipher the labels on her neatly ziplocked baggies. I hold a handful of pebbles in my hand and tilt them, watch the mica glitter in the low light of my headlamp. I can almost taste the sediment melting into my tongue, the bitter sharp of metal and the funk of dark-growing lichen, the way the rock will clatter against my teeth. I don't like to eat too much when we're in the caves but, when we get back, we'll all go out and I'll fill myself with cold beer and cheesy fries. We're getting too old for this, Sasha jokes, but she doesn't specify whether she's talking about the fries or the rest of it. That same night, Lois follows me into the bathroom and puts her hand in my pants, and a cave opens up inside of me.

A *Beginner's Guide to Cave Exploration* states that, when practiced safely, spelunking is no more dangerous than any other outdoor pursuit. Statistically speaking, twenty-eight times more fatal skiing accidents happen each year than people die as a result of caving.

But think of all the skiers who choose to fling themselves down mountains in the name of recreation. And think, then: how many spelunkers do you know? On a per capita basis, the aggregate is irrelevant.

I am the one who finds Lois, her eyes wild, her short hair thick with dark blood. The cave is quieter than I have ever heard it. Then we find Kaoli and she starts to yell, calling for help. I look at her blankly; why couldn't I do that? My mouth seems to have ossified—silent, frozen around a mouthful of invisible stones.

The paramedics come and Kaoli shows our license. Do I want to ride in the ambulance? No. I shake my head without meaning to. No, you go.

Sasha drives me home, takes my keys and unlocks the door, offers to make me some scrambled eggs, but I have figured out how to speak around the stones, send her away with a promise to text in the morning. The phone call comes only a few minutes later: Kaoli, from the hospital. Lois will be fine.

Lois will be fine, but she doesn't come back to the caves, and though we meet for coffee, the four of us, it's different above ground, as though the extra weight of the earth was some kind of atmosphere. Without stone walls around us, it's harder to talk, move, breathe. It's like I'm a cave pretending to be a person. How long have we been doing this? In the bright light of the coffee shop, I see faint wrinkles clustering around Kaoli's temples and at the corners of Sasha's mouth. Lois looks the same as ever except for the scrape on her forehead—the only sign of where she fell.

It's hard to feel surprised when Lois tells us she's moving to San Francisco. She takes up surfing, posing wet-haired in photos taken at Ocean Beach.

Scientists who study caves—there must be a name for this—have estimated that 80% of underground networks have more than one egress. What that means: only 20% of caves have an ending. The rest are like a tangled chain, a dark necklace that twists and turns below the earth's surface.

Scientists who study caves have estimated that 70% of the earth's caves are underwater. What that means: I will live out my life in 30% unless I can learn a new way to breathe.

At night, I dream a cave life for myself, a bedroom with stone walls and a four-poster of stalagmites. I dream of reaching my hands into the pockets of Lois's cargo pants and pulling out pebbles.

The only thing gayer than spelunking, I would tell Lois, is missing you.

I've been making solo expeditions. I don't tell Sasha or Kaoli because I know they'll insist on coming along— for safety, for old time's sake. But I don't want good ol' dried mango. I don't want to know which way is north.

Without the others, I move more quickly. I used to think the caves were quiet, but now, they echo with re-membered sounds: footsteps, breath. Today, today, today. My knees ache, but I keep going. After six-and-a-half hours I can sense Lois, just up ahead, around the next curve. If I can only catch up to her, I will tell her I'm ready now—ready to go deeper, ready to stay.

The Convent

The nuns were known across Europe for their preserves, which were exquisite, concocted in small batches from freshly plucked alpine fruits. In glass jars, the jams and jellies glistened on breakfast tables from Vladivostok to Copenhagen, and in the orchards around the mountain convent the nuns weighed ripe pears in their palms like full breasts.

What was preserved: the fruit, the summer sweetness of a company of women in the orchard sunshine, the memory of the sisters who had stood over the pots in the months before. In the convent kitchens, the sisters peeled and cored, chopped and macerated, practicing their witchcraft of pectin and hard work. The recipes had been passed across the years with only the slightest adjustments—a dash of nutmeg, a touch of anise, the iron taste of a drop of blood from a pricked finger.

As the moon waxed and waned over the walls of the convent, the sisters polished new jars and poured them full of curds, compotes, and marmalades. They dreamed of orchards that went on for acres, a kitchen with hundreds of pots and pans, a group of women who traveled far and wide to gather the world's bounty: the mango and the quince, the Chinese gooseberry with its fragrant scent and pale green flesh.

It happened gradually at first. A forgotten pot harden-
ing with sugar burned black. A batch of jars bursting into
shards as they were carried into the cool of the storeroom.
There were fewer of them than there had been once, for
the world outside the convent had grown tired of nuns,
and jams came now from enormous factories, where the
only song was the electrified hum of silver machines whir-
ring.

Yet the sisters were not to be dissuaded. Instead, they
brewed stronger concoctions—dark fig pastes, a cherry
jam thick with smoky spices. For so long now, they had
cast their love out from the convent in hundreds of glass
jars, offering up the fruits of their labors. For so long, they
had read from the scriptures and given their thanks for the
fruit of the tree bleeding juice against Eve's teeth. It was
true, wasn't it, that the less-perfect fruits tasted sweetest
after stewing—that there was no jostled peach or half-
squashed berry that could not be redeemed?

So they had all believed, for they were themselves the
bruised apples of the world, not loved enough by the fam-
ilies who had left them by the convent gates, the husbands
who had pushed them out when their wombs had not
borne the fruit of a human child. In the convent, every
woman had her role to play in the big, bustling kitchens,
her voice one of many raised in song along the raspberry
vines.

Now the raspberries turned rank among the brambles,
and the sisters' numbers dwindled so that matins rang thin

in the hall, and in the kitchens, pots stood cold and empty. In Vladivostok, an old woman sighed at the memory of a piece of toast she had eaten as a young woman in love, shining with plump berries. When the cherries shriveled on their branches, the sisters, now wrinkled themselves, had no choice but to empty their stores and carry the last jars up to the long wooden table that ran down one wall of the kitchen.

Something in the world had gone sour, too sour to be remedied by a spoonful of jelly—too bitter even for the nuns with their strong potions and deep, heavy pots. So they prepared the last recipe, their voices raised in a final song. Perhaps this could still preserve them, the slow stewing of the fruit, the passing of the pot from one sister to another. They waited patiently for it to cool and set, then dipped their spoons in and lifted the jam to their lips, sweet and heavy like an ending.

Acknowledgments

Versions of these stories previously appeared in the following publications:

"The Theme Park of Women's Bodies" in *The Masters Review*

"Operation Hecuba" in *Quarterly West*

"The Cure" in *Inch*

"The City," "The Convent," and "The Island" in *The Rumpus* and *The Best Small Fictions 2019*

"Red Cherry" in *Apalachee Review*

"A Lesbian's Guide to Cave Exploration" in *Hobart*

Many thanks to the editors and other hard-working staff of the publications where some of these stories originally appeared, including Julia Ridley Smith at *Inch*, Karissa Chen at *The Rumpus*, Evan Fleischer at *Hobart*, Allison Field Bell and Jesse Kohn at *Quarterly West*, Cole Meyer at *The Masters Review*, and Rafael Gamero at *Apalachee Review*. Thanks to Ross White and Noah Stetzer at Bull City Press for making my chapbook dreams come true, and Cassie Mannes Murray, publicist extraordinaire. Thanks, too, to the students of English 351 for the time they spent with this manuscript.

Thanks to my teachers, my fellow Greensboro writers, and the Werejellies of Clarion 2016. Thanks to Emily Cataneo, Grae Gardiner, and Jessie Van Rheenen for your reads and to Clare Beams and Allegra Hyde for your kind words here—and your work, which has been such a source of inspiration. Thanks to Jami Attenberg, for her #1000WordsofSummer, during which several of these stories were written.

Thanks to the person whose emails made me angry enough to consider the electrical power of rage. Thanks to the Coops for being my pirate crew. Thanks to Ash for everything.

About the Author

Maggie Cooper is a graduate of Yale College, the Clarion Writers' Workshop, and the MFA program at the University of North Carolina at Greensboro. Her writing has appeared in *The Rumpus*, *Ninth Letter*, *Inch*, and elsewhere. She lives with her spouse in the Boston area and also works as a literary agent.

This book was published with assistance from the Fall 2022 Literary Editing & Publishing class at the University of North Carolina at Chapel Hill. Contributing editors and designers were Leo Bautista, Olivia Bennett, Haleigh Cooper, Michael D'Andrea, Lauren Flors, Benjamin Foster, Emily Gajda, Sophie Hass, Helena Ketter, Emma Nelson, Diana Ortiz, Macon Porterfield, Mahitha Reddy, Micah Shaw, River Thompson, Conner Tucker, and Riley Wojcik.